STORY OF PRINCESS

THE GLOW OF MAGIC

KARTHIK

Dedicated to All Fathers and Daughters

Contents

Foreword

A daughter's relationship with their father can play a key role in their psychological development. In fact, when fathers are present in their daughters' lives, girls grow up with a healthy sense of who they are. They are more confident and self-assured and have a clearer understanding of what they want in life.

1
Chapter One

There was a Father and daughter who lived in a small village happily. There is a beautiful sea near their house. They are poor people in that village. He had one boat and he sails and lives by catching fish and selling into the market for their daily expenses.

One day the daughter asked the father also to take her to the sea. But her father scolded her and strictly said no to her because he cared for her then the daughter became upset and she stayed silent then he sat near of her daughter and by silently looked her daughter's face he felt that fear of losing her because he feared of waves.

2

Chapter Two

He thought that when he add up her daughter with him he'll lose her and he convinced and promised her that one day that he'll take her to the sea and his daughter became so happy and he went to the sea for Fishing.

Surprisingly He found one beautiful enormous "precious pearl"

He arrived home eagerly with so much joy to show her daughter that he found a beautiful Pearle to give her Pearl as his token of love.

He ran to her and asked to close her eyes.She closed her eyes with a smile and he took a Pearl in his hand and he said to open the eyes.

His daughter was so happy to saw the pearl for the first time she jumped in joy and she took the pearl in her hand and She always

carried that pearl with her.

One fine morning she

was very curious to see the sea because she thought that she could find so many pearls like this at that time her father took her to the sea she was wondering how beautiful these sea waves are she asked her father

"Daddy"
what is there over the sea?

He answered There is a lots of beautiful pearls like you my daughter and they both laughed with so much of happiness on that time one big wave came near their boat and the wave eaten up her daughter she drowned with the pearl into the sea and He lost her daughter.

3

Chapter Three

He worried and cried that he did wrong thing today and He asked God to give his daughter back.

But God didn't heard his word.He returned to his with so much of sorrow Days passed away He

became sick without eating any food one day he cried alot and slept.

He dreamed like that his daughter is still alive Suddenly he got woken up and searched for his boat unfortunately he forgot that his boat got damaged in that accident.

Then he sold all the fish and his own home for the money to get a new boat for searching for his daughter.

4

Chapter Four

He went to shop and bought new boat and he returned with hope that he will get his daughter back.

He arrived at sea and started to sail his boat by calling her daughter's name loudly he crossed

quarter sea with full of tears But he was tired to sail the boat whenever he closes his eye his daughter's face will come in front of him so he didn't gave up again he started to sail the boat now he reached middle of the ocean he see four side water surrounded by him and no one is there presence even to help him Now this time God watched his suffering and decided to help him.

5

Chapter Five

Suddenly some bright light came from centre of the sea.

He felt that could be the light of pearl with full of expectations that something good going to be happen..the bright god's grace pearl light came out of the sea with his daughter He felt thankful to god with full of happy tears..and the pearl light sounded like I'm

"The Pearl God"

Who lives in the sea..You found me and took with yourself to give me as a token of love at that time I felt I'm not precious as much your love for you daughter that time from that day.

I was happy to be with you and with your daughter like one of your family member..The Pearl God said I still wanted to be with you two people.. don't worry now I'll give your home back...hereafter I'll took care of you both and the light fade away and change into a beautiful Pearl

as early one and the father and daughter went the home Happily with a pearl..And then their life changed into rich and healthy..They both lived their happily and peacefully by god's

grace.

6
Chapter Six

But recent research has shown that a father's influence in his daughter's life shapes her self-esteem, self-image, confidence and opinions of men. A girl's relationship with her dad can determine her ability to trust, her need for approval and her self-belief. It can even affect her love life.

7
Chapter Seven

Her "First Love"

How a father treats both his daughter and her mother can help a young woman feel safe and secure in her relationships with the boys and men in her life, including her future husband.

8
Chapter Eight

Respect her uniqueness.

Urge her to love her body and discourage dieting. Make sure your daughter knows that you love her for who she is. See her as a whole person capable of doing anything. Treat her and those she loves with respect.

9

Honestly i Dedicated to All fathers and daughters

Happy Ending
"Nothing is precious than pure love"

About The Author

Hi,

I'm Karthik, and I believe that people have far more potential than they give themselves credit for.

I believe that everyone can find their calling, achieve success and happiness, and feel in control of their fate.

Through my writing, I hope to educate and inspire, to convince people to look at themselves and the world a little differently, and to be able to use these insights to improve not only their lives, but the lives of everyone they touch as well.

If that floats your boat, I think you'll like my work, and I hope you find it helpful.

Thank you all,

CONTACT US :

Mail Support :
Karthikrichie1305@outlook.com
Karthikrichie1305@gmail.com
Whatsapp Support :
+91 8148147901

www.ingramcontent.com/pod-product-compliance
Lightning Source LLC
Chambersburg PA
CBHW021200130726
47988CB00004B/1702